CW00847986

A Place
to Call Home

by Jenn MacCormack

illustrated by
Peipei

This book belongs to:

_____

This book is for all the
children who choose to follow
their dreams rather
than the crowd.

There once was a little duck named Mally.

He had everything a duck could ever want.
He was wild and free, and his home in the sky was filled with endless adventures.

But, Mally was sad.

The ducks had just finished migration.
It was a long journey and Mally was EXHAUSTED!

"PHEW," said Mally, "I think I want to RETIRE!"

"RETIRE?! What does *that* mean?" asked the other ducks confusingly.

"I don't want to migrate anymore," replied Mally sadly. The other ducks burst out laughing.

"Silly Mally," they quacked, "We HAVE to migrate! That's just the way things are!"

Mally felt *worse* than he did before. He didn't *like* the way things were. It hurt his feelings when his friends laughed at him.

The next morning,
Mally decided to fly towards
the sunrise to find a place
where he wouldn't have to
migrate anymore.

A place he could call home.

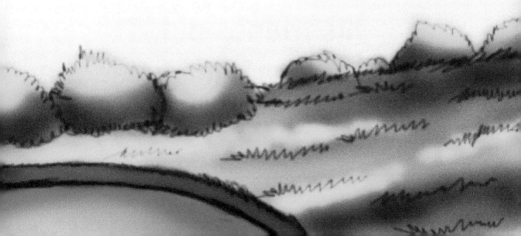

Mally flew for hours and rested at a nearby park. The birds noticed he was new to the area, so they asked where he was headed.

"I am looking for a home where I can retire from migrating," he replied nervously.

He was afraid these birds would laugh at him just like his friends did.
"I know a place," answered the swan.

"It's a place called Wentworth Park on the island of Cape Breton," said the swan. "Hundreds of ducks live there all year long."

"That sounds perfect," sighed Mally happily.

"Fly east until you come to a long road on the sea. From there, the lighthouse birds will explain the rest of the way."

Mally was *so* excited he almost forgot to say "thank you"!
He hugged the swan and flew off to search for the road on the sea.

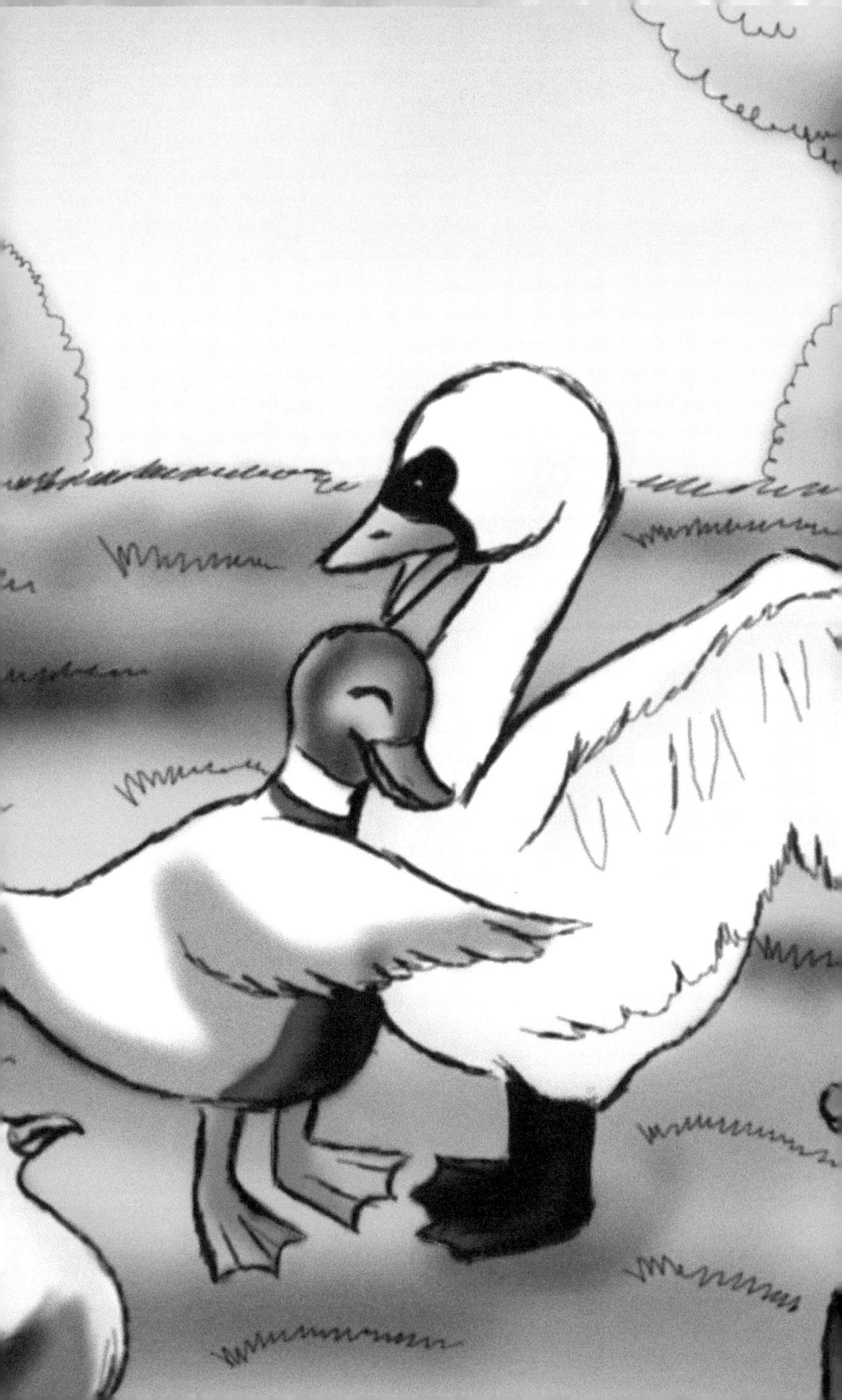

Mally flew, and flew, and FLEW until he saw a long road on the sea.

He was getting CLOSER!

He was fascinated to see a bridge that swung open to let a ship pass through.

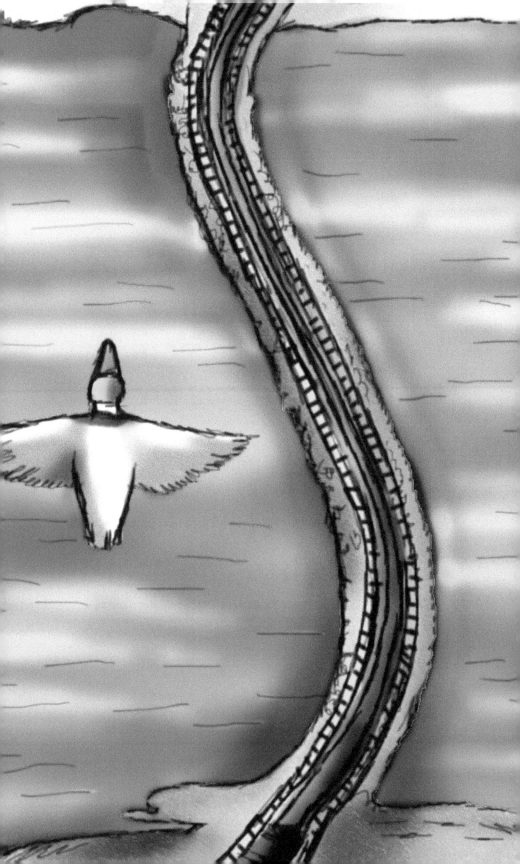

Mally took a rest at the
swing bridge.
He read the sign:
"Welcome to Cape Breton."

Mally smiled. That sign made
his heart feel like he was
actually heading home!

Mally noticed the lighthouse birds just past the swing bridge. He flew over and asked if they knew how to get to Wentworth Park.

"I do," replied one duck, "My grandfather retired there!"

Mally listened carefully to the directions, thanked the duck, and quickly flew towards Sydney.

He saw a little ice cream shop called, *"The Tasty Treat"* so he decided to stop and rest.

Some humans gave him a bite of their ice cream.

Oooooo, that was cold! It made his brain FREEZE!

As Mally flew over Sydney, he saw a large cruise ship in the harbour.

The dock was filled with people and he could hear music!

The music was actually coming from the LARGEST fiddle he had ever SEEN! He couldn't resist taking a break in front of it.

It was then Mally noticed someone was taking his picture!!

"CHEESE!" said Mally, just as the man's camera sounded. Click-click-SNAP!!

Finally, Mally landed at Wentworth Park - and the swan was right!
There were **HUNDREDS** of ducks!

Mally quickly waddled down the path and joined them in the water.

He looked around and smiled.
He really *WAS* wild and free now!
NO MORE MIGRATING!!!

He was SO happy he finally found a place to call HOME...

...on the beautiful Cape Breton Island.